Magic Pony Carousel
Book 6

CRYSTAL
THE SNOW PONY

Magic Pony Carousel
Book 6

CRYSTAL
THE SNOW PONY

Poppy Shire

Illustrations by Ron Berg

HarperTrophy®

An Imprint of HarperCollins*Publishers*

★ ★ ★ ★ ★

CRYSTAL THE SNOW PONY

Text copyright © 2008 by Working Partners

www.harpercollinschildrens.com

Library of Congress Cataloging-in-Publication Data
Shire, Poppy.
    Crystal the snow pony / Poppy Shire ; illustrations by Ron Berg.
    —1st ed.
        p.   cm. — (Magic pony carousel ; bk. 6)
    Summary: Emily goes for a ride on a magic carousel that takes
her to the snowy mountains, where she and her pony, Crystal, try
to save a village from an avalanche and track down a boy who has
run away.
    ISBN 978-0-06-083791-4 (pbk. bdg.)
    [1. Runaways—Fiction. 2. Avalanches—Fiction. 3. Ponies—
Fiction. 4. Space and time—Fiction. 5. Magic—Fiction.] I. Berg,
Ron, ill. II. Title.
PZ7.S55795Cry 2008   2008000770
[Fic]—dc22   CIP
                                                      AC

Typography by Sasha Illingworth
❖
First Edition
★ ★ ★ ★ ★

With special thanks to Holly Skeet

Magic Pony Carousel
Book 6

CRYSTAL
THE SNOW PONY

Chapter One

Emily was so excited, she could hardly breathe. The fairground was filled with colors and sounds, and she couldn't wait to try some of the fantastic rides. She turned slowly on the spot, wondering which ride to go on first.

"Come on, Emily! Max has spotted an airplane ride." Emily's big sister, Jane, was calling her. Jane had brought Emily and Max to the fair as a treat. They'd been looking forward to it for ages.

"Coming!" Emily called back, running after her sister. The airplanes didn't look very exciting to her, but maybe that was because she was eight and Max was only five. Jane helped Max into one of the blue and yellow planes. As the ride swooped around he made "neeeoow" noises and pretended to talk to the control tower. He was very disappointed when it stopped, so Emily suggested getting some cotton candy.

"I don't want any cotton candy!" Max wailed. "I want to go on the airplanes again!"

"But this is the only ride we've seen! The others will be fun, too," Emily promised.

"Noooo! This one, this one, this one!" Max's face turned bright red as he got ready to have one of his tantrums.

"Okay!" Jane said. "You can have one more ride on the plane. Just one, remember!"

Max beamed, and Emily sighed. Max always got his own way because he was the youngest. She had a feeling that just one more ride wouldn't be enough for her little brother.

Luckily Max felt so dizzy after his second spin on the airplane that he didn't protest when Emily and Jane said they wanted to find some different rides.

Emily led the way through the fairground, holding one of Max's sticky hands. What should she go on? The superslide? The bumper cars?

Suddenly she heard a lovely tune playing in the distance. It was almost as if the music was calling her! She pulled Max and Jane along behind her as she followed the tinkling notes.

"Oh look!" Emily gasped.

The music was coming from an old-fashioned carousel, painted in sparkling red and gold. The colors flashed as it twirled merrily around. Emily thought she'd never seen anything so beautiful.

All three of them stopped. "It's so pretty!" said Emily. "Jane, please may I have a ride on that?"

Jane laughed. "Of course you can."

The carousel slowed down and the music faded away. Emily ran over to look at the ponies. She admired a lovely dapple-gray circus pony with twinkling eyes and a dashing Arabian with a flowing mane. Then she spotted a gorgeous pony the color of caramel ice cream that she recognized from her pony magazines. It was a snow rescue pony! Snow rescue ponies were used in mountain countries for traveling in deep snow. They were Emily's favorite kind of pony! They looked different from other ponies, with their small bodies. She loved the way they had a cute black stripe running from the top of their head all the way down their back.

The wooden pony had a kind face. Emily climbed the steps to the carousel and stroked the pony's neck. His leather bridle had little silver bells jingling on it, tied with bunches of yellow

ribbon. His coat looked soft and furry—Emily knew it had to be very thick to keep him warm through snowy winters. She ran her hand down the pony's mane. It stood straight up, just like a zebra's. She noticed he had faint zebra stripes on his legs, too.

A booming voice behind Emily startled her. "Hello there! Are you admiring my mountain pony?"

Emily turned around to find a sparkly-eyed gentleman in a green velvet suit standing beside the carousel. "He's beautiful!" Emily said, running down the steps to stand beside him.

The carousel owner raised his green-striped top hat to Emily and bowed low. "I'm Mr. Barker and this is my Magic Pony Carousel. Would you like to have a ride on one of my ponies?" he asked.

Emily nodded. "Yes, please!"

Mr. Barker rubbed his hands together, then blew on them hard. "Brrrr! It's chilly today, don't you think? Winter's on its way." He opened his hands again, revealing a little pile of pink tickets cupped in his palms.

Emily stared in astonishment. Where had all those pink tickets come from?

"Take a ticket, my dear!" said Mr. Barker. "The name of your pony will be written on it."

Emily reached for the corner of a pink ticket that was poking out from the pile. She really wanted to ride the snow rescue pony! She unfolded the ticket with trembling fingers. In swirly black writing it read *Crystal*.

She looked hopefully up at Mr. Barker, and he nodded at the carousel. "Take a look!" he said.

Emily climbed up onto the carousel again. All the ponies had a little name plate attached to the pole in front of their saddles. She peered up to read the caramel-colored pony's name. *Crystal!* It was the perfect name for a snow pony!

"Thank you!" she said to Mr. Barker. "He's exactly the pony I wanted to ride!"

Mr. Barker smiled, and Emily scrambled onto Crystal's back. His saddle was made of heavy leather. Underneath it was a beautiful dark red saddlecloth, embroidered with tiny flowers and leaves in twinkling gold thread. Emily felt so safe on Crystal's back.

Mr. Barker stood in the middle of the carousel and twirled a golden handle. The tinkling tune played once more, and Emily laughed out loud as she felt Crystal swoop into the air. She waved to Jane and Max, who were watching her, and they waved back.

The carousel began to spin faster, and the fairground became a blur of laughing faces. Everything started to disappear in a rainbow mist.

Emily blinked. She wanted to rub her eyes, but they were going so fast, she didn't dare let go of Crystal's reins. Silvery sparkles whirled around her, and the rainbow colors of the fairground changed to dazzling white. Everything shone and glittered with light, and Emily gasped out loud.

This wasn't the fairground anymore. She and Crystal were in the middle of a snowstorm!

Chapter Two

The snowflakes faded away and Emily gazed around, utterly confused. What had happened to Jane and Max and the fair? Now she was in a valley, surrounded by glistening fields of pure white snow. Huge craggy mountains rose up sharply on either side, their peaks topped with even more snow. It was just getting dark, and the sky was a beautiful deep velvety blue.

Crystal tossed his head, making the bells on his reins jingle loudly. The sound echoed around the valley: *jingle, jangle, ting, ting.*

Emily stared down at her pony in astonishment. He wasn't made of wood anymore. He was real!

"What's going on?" Emily asked in wonder. She ran her hand down Crystal's black-and-cream mane. Stiff bristly hairs tickled her fingers. When she touched his neck, it felt warm and furry.

Emily shivered. It was *really* cold. Her favorite embroidered jeans and pink denim jacket weren't much use here. But when Emily looked down at what she was wearing, she saw that her clothes had changed! Now she was dressed in thick, warm slacks of cherry-red corduroy. They were tucked into cozy sheepskin boots, tied with strings with gorgeous little bobbles. She also wore a green felt coat, embroidered with cherry-red flowers around the collar and cuffs. Beautiful sheepskin gloves dangled on strings from each

sleeve. Emily pulled them on and wriggled her fingers in the cozy fleece. This was a perfect outfit for the snowy weather.

But they couldn't stay out here forever. It was getting dark. Emily nudged Crystal's sides with her heels, and he trotted forward. Once Emily was used to rising up and down to his bouncy trot, she looked around to see where they were going.

The road led to a little mountain village. Warm yellow lights twinkled in the windows of the sturdy log cabins. Smoke puffed from the chimneys, filling the air with a sharp woody tang.

"It's just like a Christmas card!" Emily said in delight.

The thick carpet of snow made everything very quiet. No one seemed to be around, and Emily wondered where all the people could be.

"What should I do?" she said, thinking out loud.

"I think we should head for the village square," a voice replied.

Emily nearly fell out of the saddle in surprise. Who said that? She stood up in her stirrups and stared around, but there was no one in sight. Crystal's ears flicked back at her. Was someone playing a trick?

"I must have imagined it," Emily decided, sitting back down.

"No, you didn't!" said the voice.

Crystal snorted and turned his head to look at Emily. His brown eyes shone merrily.

Emily leaned forward to whisper in his ear. "Did you say that?" she asked. She felt a bit silly talking to a pony.

"Of course I did!" replied Crystal. His breath billowed out in a steamy cloud. "Come on. It's much too cold to stay outside. I've got my extra thick coat to keep me warm, but even your winter clothes won't be enough in this weather." He set off again at a brisk trot.

"But, Crystal, you have to tell me what's happening! Where are we? Why have you turned into a real pony? How can you *talk*?"

"All ponies can talk," Crystal explained. "But you can understand me, because you were given the magic ticket for the carousel. It sent us here for a special reason. We found each other through the magic and now we've got a task to do. But don't worry, you'll be back before anyone notices you're gone. That's part of the magic, too!"

Emily patted Crystal's neck. This was so exciting! "What sort of task is it?"

"I'm not sure yet. We've come to help someone, but I don't know who. We'll know when we find the right person, don't worry!"

There was a crackling noise ahead, and Emily could see showers of orange sparks shooting into the dark sky. They rounded a corner to see a big bonfire in the middle of the village square. There were lots of people standing around it, talking and laughing.

Emily smiled. "Well, we've certainly got plenty of people to choose from!"

She took her feet out of the stirrups and slithered down from Crystal's back. "We'd better not talk anymore," she whispered in his ear, "or they'll hear us."

"It's all right," Crystal murmured back. "No one else can understand me. Only you have the carousel magic. Everyone else will just hear me whinnying or see me twitching my nose."

It was just as well that no one else could hear Crystal, because at that very moment, someone

close behind Emily called out, "Hello!"

Emily turned to see a girl of her own age smiling at her. She was wearing a blue corduroy coat covered in embroidered flowers and curling tendrils of leaves. Her white-blond hair was twisted into two long braids, tied with bright blue ribbon. A little boy with the same fine blond hair was holding her hand.

"Hi there," said the girl. "I'm Sasha, and this is my brother, Arin."

"I'm Emily," said Emily. "And this is Crystal, my pony."

"He's gorgeous! But you look cold." Sasha sounded concerned. "Why don't you come near the fire and warm up?" She led the way through the crowd toward the bonfire. Suddenly the little boy slipped his hand out of his sister's. He dashed off, weaving between people's legs.

Sasha gasped a quick "Sorry!" and shot after him.

Emily shook her head. "Arin's just like Max! That's my brother," she explained to Crystal. "He's always running off, getting me and Jane in trouble."

Emily stepped a little closer to the flames to warm her hands while she waited for Sasha to come back. On the other side of the fire, several children were dancing in a circle. They were holding birch twigs with feathers tied on them.

"Why are they carrying twigs?" Emily whispered to Crystal.

"It must be Spring Festival," Crystal replied. "This is how the villagers say good-bye to winter. The birch twigs have green buds on them to show that spring is coming. And feathers are used to represent flowers because there aren't many real flowers out yet."

"They're so pretty. Oh look, there's Sasha!" said Emily.

Sasha was stomping toward them, dragging Arin.

"I want to go and play with my friends," Arin whined.

"Well, you can't! Mother told me to look after you."

Arin stopped pulling at his sister's arm and looked as if he was going to follow her quietly. But as soon as she turned around, he snatched his hand away and made a run for it.

Sasha dived after him. "Arin, come back!"

Crystal swung his head around into Arin's path and gently brought the little boy to a stop.

Sasha looked very annoyed. "Arin! Why do you have to keep running off? You know Mother said you were to stay with me!"

Arin shrugged, kicking his boot in the snow. Crystal snuffled his hair, and the little boy's face broke into a smile. "I like your pony," he told Emily. "What are you doing in our village? Have you come to visit someone?"

Emily gulped. What on earth was she going to say?

Chapter Three

Emily shot a panicked glance at Crystal. She couldn't ask him out loud what she should tell them. Sasha and Arin would think she was crazy! She thought quickly, and the children dancing around with their birch twigs gave her an idea.

"I've come to visit for the Spring Festival," she said. She changed the subject before Arin asked any more difficult questions. "Would you like to stroke Crystal, Arin? He's very friendly."

Arin nodded. He dug a hand into his pocket

and pulled out an apple. He held it on the flat of his palm, and Crystal crunched it up. "I could get used to this," Crystal murmured happily, putting his head down so that Arin could scratch behind his ears.

"It's getting quite late," said Sasha. "We should be going home soon before the snow starts again." She turned to Emily. "Do you have somewhere to stay?"

Emily shook her head, suddenly feeling worried. It was getting very dark. Would she and Crystal have to stay outside all night?

"Would you like to stay with us?" asked Sasha. "I'm sure my parents wouldn't mind. There's room for Crystal in our stable, and you could sleep in the top bunk of my bed."

Emily beamed. "Thank you! We'd love to."

"Let's go," said Sasha. Still firmly holding

Arin's hand, she started to walk out of the village square. "Look, it's starting to snow," she said a little anxiously.

Emily looked up. The sky had clouded over, and heavy flakes were drifting to the ground. They drifted onto Crystal's thick coat and melted away almost at once, leaving him covered in sparkling drops.

Emily blinked as a snowflake landed on her eyelashes. She'd never seen snow fall so thickly before. "I'm glad we're staying with Sasha tonight," she whispered to Crystal. The pony nodded and tossed his head, scattering snowflakes from his mane.

Sasha and Arin's house was on the side of the village farthest away from the mountains. "My parents are cattle herders," Sasha explained, "so we live close to the meadows where the cows stay." As they walked through the village, Sasha pointed out different buildings to Emily—the school, the church, and the village hall, which was being rebuilt and looked more like a wooden skeleton than a hall.

Emily could hardly take everything in. She just kept staring at the mountains towering above them.

Sasha laughed. "Haven't you ever seen a mountain before?"

"The mountains aren't so big where I live," Emily said, thinking fast. "But I wasn't really looking at the mountain—I was watching all that snow. It's falling so thickly!"

Sasha nodded. "Yes, we should get home— this is turning into a real blizzard. We're nearly there. . . ."

Emily was starting to feel cold again, and the

snow was falling so thickly she could hardly see where they were going. Now that they were out of the shelter of the town square, the wind was stronger. Icy snowflakes stung her cheeks and clung to her eyelashes.

"Shelter behind me," said Crystal. He was trudging along with his head down and his eyes half closed. His face was almost white from snowflakes, and the saddle was hidden under a crisp, frosty blanket. "I think we're going in circles, Emily." He sniffed at the wind. "Sasha must have lost her way in the snow."

Just then Sasha stopped, a frightened look on her face. She whispered to Emily so Arin wouldn't hear. "Emily, I think we've gone wrong! It's such a short distance, but the snow—I can't see. . . ."

"I think Crystal might be able to guide us,"

Emily said, trying to sound brave and gazing hopefully into Crystal's face. He stood still for a moment, feeling the wind and tasting the air. Then he nudged Emily gently with his chin. "Put your arm around my neck. Tell Sasha, too. I can follow the scent of the cattle. But this is a bad storm and I can't risk losing any of you. Arin had better ride—he's too little to trek through this."

Emily explained all this to Sasha, and together they lifted Arin up. He was delighted to ride. Then they set off again, the two girls leaning close to Crystal as they plowed on.

Suddenly a dark shape loomed ahead of them, with squares of yellow light shining through the snow. As they drew nearer, Emily realized it was a log cabin, with smaller wooden buildings at one side.

"We're home!" cried Arin.

"You star, Crystal!" Emily murmured in his ear. "I can't believe you did it!"

Crystal snorted. "Nothing to it," he murmured, but he sounded proud of himself.

"Emily, thank you! I was so scared! Come on, the stable is this way." Sasha took Emily's arm to guide her. "My pony, Clover, will keep Crystal company tonight."

Sasha pushed open the door to a barn. Inside, a pretty chestnut pony with a white splash on her nose stood knee-deep in a bed of thick straw. She whinnied happily when she saw Crystal.

Emily took off Crystal's saddle and bridle, shook the snow off, and placed them on hooks beside the door. Crystal went over to Clover, and they touched noses. Emily looked around the stable. It seemed very cozy, but she was still worried that Crystal would be cold in the night.

Sasha noticed her worried face. "It's all right, Emily. Crystal will be fine. He's got lots of hay to eat, so he can keep himself warm. But we'll put a blanket over him, too."

Arin fetched a heavy dark blue blanket from a chest by the wall, and the two girls unfolded it over Crystal's back, buckling it under his tummy.

"Have you brought guests back from the bonfire, Sasha?" asked a friendly voice. A kind-looking man with twinkly eyes was leaning against the door.

"Emily, this is Gregor," said Sasha. "He helps my father with the farm. Emily's visiting for Spring Festival, Gregor. I was just telling her that her pony will be warm enough. He'll be fine, won't he?"

"Definitely. You're a beautiful boy, aren't you?" Gregor stroked Crystal's neck. He smiled at Emily.

Emily couldn't help thinking she knew him from somewhere—his smile seemed very familiar. In fact, he looked a lot like Mr. Barker from the fair! Surely those were the same twinkling eyes? Gregor winked at her.

Before Emily could say anything, the door to the stable opened, and the most enormous dog she had ever seen slid through the gap. He was almost as big as Crystal, with shaggy dark gray fur. Emily gasped.

"Ivar!" cried Arin in delight. He stood on tiptoe and flung his arms around the dog's neck. The dog licked Arin's ear with a long pink tongue.

"Ivar sleeps in the stable, too. He's too big to

sleep in the house!" Sasha explained. "Oh! Did you hear that? Mother's calling us for dinner. Come on, Arin."

"No! I'm playing with Ivar. Go away, Sasha!" Arin dodged around his sister and ran to the corner of the stable, where he disappeared on a path that sloped down under the floor.

Emily stared in surprise. Where had Arin gone? Crystal looked puzzled, too, with his head held up and his ears pricked.

Gregor chuckled. "He's hiding in the apple cellar again. Well, I've got to be off. Nice to meet you, Emily—and you, Crystal." He winked once more, then let himself out of the barn.

With a sigh, Sasha ran down the slope after her brother. Emily followed her, stopping halfway down the path. At the bottom, she could see a dark little room that stretched away under the floor. It was full of apples, and the air was filled with a sweet, fruity scent.

Sasha came back, pulling Arin behind her. "Sorry about that, Emily. Let's go and have dinner."

Emily gave Crystal one more hug. "Sleep well," he whispered to her. "Remember, we've got to find our special task in the morning!"

The farmhouse was as warm and cozy as the stable, and the smell of the wooden walls reminded Emily of Christmas trees. She'd never stayed in a log cabin before!

Sasha's mother bustled around the kitchen. She seemed very pleased to meet Emily. "Sit down, sit down! Make yourself at home. You look frozen," she scolded gently as she fetched a plate to lay an extra place at the table. Then she went over to the stove to stir a steaming pot of stew.

The stew was delicious, and it warmed Emily right down to her toes. As she finished off the bowl she could feel her eyelids drooping.

"Do you want to come and see where you'll be sleeping?" Sasha asked.

"Yes, please." Emily stood up, trying not to yawn. "Thank you for the lovely meal, and for letting me stay," she said to Sasha's parents.

As she followed Sasha to the stairs that led out of the kitchen, she peeked through the shutters at the window. There was a tiny window in the stable wall next to the farmhouse, and Emily could see Crystal and Clover munching their hay together. They looked very comfortable.

Sasha led Emily into her parents' room, which had a big double bed in the middle, covered with blue knitted blankets. A narrow wooden ladder was fixed to the wall on the far side of the bed. Sasha went over and started to scramble up the ladder. "Come on," she called over her shoulder, and Emily followed her, popping her head up through a trapdoor into the sweetest little attic bedroom.

There were red and white quilts on the bunk beds and a warm furry rug on the floor. Sasha lent Emily a thick cotton nightgown, and she pulled it over her head before clambering sleepily into the top bunk.

"Good night, Emily," Sasha called from the bottom bunk.

"Sleep tight," Emily replied. As she burrowed her cheek into the soft pillow, she glanced out of the window. Through a chink in the curtains she could see the dark sky, patterned with snowflakes. The wind had died down, and the air was filled with fluffy flakes drifting gently to the ground.

Emily sighed happily. This was the best adventure she had ever had. She couldn't wait for tomorrow!

Chapter Four

"Wake up! Wake up!"

Someone was shaking Emily's shoulder. "Go away, Max!" she muttered.

"Who's Max? I'm not Max, I'm Arin! Come on, it's time to get up!" Arin was standing on the steps of the bunk bed and had reached across to shake Emily awake.

"Arin! You know you're not allowed up here." Sasha shooed her little brother back down the ladder.

Emily scrambled out of bed and stretched

her arms. Tiny specks of dust danced in the sunbeams that slanted through the window. It had stopped snowing, and the sky was clear and blue.

Sasha smiled at Emily. "Do you want to come for a pony ride today? I'd like to show you one of my favorite places."

Emily nodded. "That sounds lovely," she said.

"I want to come, too!" Arin shouted up the ladder.

"No, Arin! You're too little. You have to stay with Mother today."

Emily could hear Arin stomping downstairs, complaining. Sasha started to get dressed. "Come on! Let's go while the sun is shining. We'll grab some bread and cheese on our way out."

The two girls shot downstairs, wrapped up some bread in a handkerchief, and said good-bye to Sasha's mother. Then they ran out to the stable, leaving Arin wailing behind them. "Please let me come! I'll be good, I promise!"

"No, you have to stay here, Arin!" Sasha called. She rolled her eyes at Emily. "Little brothers can be such a nuisance!"

"I know," Emily agreed.

Crystal seemed very pleased to see her when she went into the stable. He tossed his head and blew gently into her hair. Emily gave him a hug, then took off his blanket and put on his heavy leather saddle over the red saddlecloth. Clover had a saddle like Crystal's, but her saddlecloth was green. She didn't have bells on her bridle, either.

Soon the ponies were trotting through the town toward the mountain. As they left the meadows, the path grew steeper and rockier, and the ponies slowed down to pick their way

carefully over the stones.

Emily let Sasha and Clover get a little way in front. Then she leaned forward and whispered in Crystal's ear. "Do you think it's all right to go riding like this?" she asked. "Shouldn't we concentrate on finding who the magic carousel wants us to help?"

"Don't worry." Crystal gave a cheerful whinny. "The magic will make sure we find out what we're supposed to do."

"Oh look!" Sasha gave a shout from up ahead.

"What is it?" Emily asked, craning her neck to see. Sasha was pointing at something on the ground by a ring of tall silver birch trees.

"Do you see that patch of blue? They're gentians—spring flowers, Emily!"

The gentians looked like little scraps of deepest blue paper peeping through the melting snow. They were beautiful, but Emily was a bit puzzled that Sasha was so excited.

Sasha scrambled out of Clover's saddle to kneel by the flowers for a closer look. "These are the first ones I've seen this year! That means spring is nearly here. I'll have to tell everyone we've seen the gentians when we get back."

She got back on Clover, and the girls carried on up the path, spotting more flowers. Some were blue, like the gentians, while others were pale yellow and creamy white, a bit like snowdrops. As they rode deeper among the trees, the air filled with the sound of dripping water. *Drip, drip, drip.*

Emily looked up. The snow was melting off the branches. Emily yelped as a cold droplet went down the back of her neck. Drops splashed onto Crystal's mane, resting on the black hair like gleaming jewels.

"Come on!" Sasha called, pushing Clover into a brisk trot. "There's the cat rock! It's not far to my secret place now." She pointed to a rock by the path that really did look like a cat, with two pointy ears and a lump on its back that could have been a tail curled up.

The path grew narrower and more overgrown. Although she wasn't cold inside her thick clothes, Emily shivered. It looked as if no one had been this way for ages!

Finally they stopped at a wall of gleaming gray stone that sloped steeply up the side of the mountain. Sasha slid out of the saddle and tied Clover's reins to a tree branch. She turned to face Emily, one hand resting on the shining stone.

"I found this a few weeks ago," Sasha explained. "Isn't it beautiful? It's a frozen waterfall!"

Emily looked closer at the cliff. It wasn't made

of stone at all. It was a giant sheet of ice! She jumped off Crystal's back and tied his reins to the same branch as Clover's.

But when she turned around, Sasha had vanished!

Emily's heart started to pound. Where was Sasha? She stared into the trees, noticing how quiet and lonely this place was. "Sasha? Sasha, where are you?" she called.

Suddenly she caught a movement out of the corner of her eye. She spun around and gasped in shock. There in the waterfall—*inside the ice*—was Sasha!

Chapter Five

Suddenly Sasha popped out from behind the wall of frozen water and waved at Emily.

"How did you do that?" Emily gasped. "You were *inside* the waterfall!"

Sasha beamed. "Not exactly. I told you my secret place was special, didn't I? Come and see." She beckoned, so Emily ran along the path to where she was standing.

The sheet of silvery ice stretched up beside them, but there was a gap between the wall of ice and the mountainside behind it. "Come on!" Sasha beckoned once more, then slid into the gap.

Emily took a deep breath and followed her. Behind the frozen waterfall, the mountainside arched away to form a large rocky cave. The dappled light of the forest changed to a pale, watery glimmer as it filtered through the thick sheet of clear, greenish ice. It was like being underwater. Emily laughed in delight.

"Come and see this!" called Sasha, who was standing at the back of the cave.

The floor of the cave was rocky and uneven so Emily kept one hand on the wall for balance as she walked over to Sasha. Suddenly she noticed strange patterns under her gloves, delicate swirling lines in all different colors. "Sasha, look! The walls are painted!"

"I know! Aren't they beautiful? I think they are paintings of Spring Festival—there are people dancing over here, surrounded by pictures of flowers." She stood on tiptoe and pointed to some dark blue splashes. "See, those are gentians, like the ones we saw. I wonder if the painters used squashed-up gentian petals for the color. I don't know how old the paintings are. They're probably ancient."

Emily nodded. Then she peered more closely at the cave wall. One of the shapes was bigger than the rest, painted in light brown with four stubby legs.

"It's a pony, just like Crystal!" Emily cried. She pulled off one of her gloves and traced her finger around the shape. The small, delicate head and spiky mane were exactly like Crystal's!

They followed the paintings along the wall, spotting more flowers and different animals. Eventually, Sasha said, "We ought to get back. It'll be time for lunch soon."

Emily stood in the middle of the cave and took one last look around. "Thanks so much for bringing me here, Sasha. It's the most beautiful place I've ever seen. I never dreamed I'd walk behind a waterfall!"

They went back out to Crystal and Clover, who were happily munching sweet mountain grass. Even though the wind was still cold, it felt much warmer out in the bright sunshine. It was strange to hear the sound of dripping water and birds singing after the quiet cave.

"I've just got to tighten Clover's girth," Sasha said. "It felt a bit loose as we were coming up." She started to fiddle with the leather strap.

Emily stroked Crystal's ears. "There was a pony just like you painted on the cave wall," she whispered.

Crystal tossed his head, as if he was pleased. "I'm thirsty," he said. "Is there anywhere around here to have a drink?"

Emily noticed a pool of melted water at the foot of the waterfall. Drops were still running down the sheet of ice into the pool, and Emily wondered how much longer the waterfall would stay frozen. She led Crystal over to the water so he could drink.

But Crystal just stood there with his ears back.

"What's wrong?" Emily asked. "Aren't you thirsty anymore?"

"There shouldn't be so much water here," Crystal muttered, looking up at the waterfall.

"Why not?" said Emily.

Crystal gave her a worried look. "The waterfall shouldn't be melting this early. The weather must be warmer than usual, which explains why all the flowers are out. I think the spring thaw is happening too fast!"

Crystal's voice was so serious that Emily felt anxious, too. "What does that mean?"

"If snow melts too quickly, it can be dangerous. All the snow that fell yesterday could turn into an avalanche!"

Emily caught her breath. She'd read about avalanches. They were great falls of snow that rushed suddenly down mountains. They could bury people or even whole towns!

Emily turned to see where Sasha was. They had to get back to the village! She opened her mouth to call out, but Crystal nudged her. "Don't shout, Emily. Loud noises can set an avalanche off."

Quickly Emily led him back over to Sasha, who was tugging at Clover's girth to make sure they were tight enough. She turned and grinned at Emily. "Ready to go?"

"Yes. But, Sasha, listen. I'm worried. Did

you see that big pool of water at the bottom of the waterfall? The spring thaw's happening very fast. . . ."

Sasha looked at the water and then at the dripping trees along the path. Her rosy cheeks paled till her face was as white as her blond hair. "Emily, you're right! We must get back to the town and warn everybody. There could be an avalanche!"

Chapter Six

The girls trotted back down the mountain as quickly as they could. Emily clung tightly to Crystal's mane as he plunged through the snow and scrambled over loose stones. They reached the village square just before lunchtime. The sun shone brightly down on the people bustling about.

Just as the girls were about to blurt out their warning, Emily noticed Crystal's ears twitch. Then he laid them flat back along his head as if he was scared. Emily stroked his neck. "What's the matter, Crystal?"

"We're too late. I can hear an avalanche coming!"

Emily gave a gasp of horror. They hadn't had a chance to warn anyone! She could hear it now, too—a dull rumbling sound like thunder, growing louder all the time. Emily stared up at the mountain. There was a faint white mist hanging near the peak—far above Sasha's cave. Was it a cloud, or was it snow plunging down toward the village?

She looked at Sasha and knew she had heard the avalanche, too. She was even whiter than before. "Avalanche!" she shouted, cantering Clover right into the middle of the square. "Run!"

The villagers started to panic, dashing around like startled hens. "Avalanche!" shouted someone. "An avalanche is coming!"

"The village is right in the path of the

avalanche," Crystal said grimly. "Everyone needs to leave at once."

"But where will we go?" Emily asked him. "Oh, Crystal, we should have warned everyone sooner. I'm so sorry!"

"We came back as fast as we could," said Crystal. "I don't think we've found our task yet."

They had to stop talking then because Sasha and Clover cantered over to them. "We normally shelter in the village hall," she explained, "but it's being rebuilt. There's nowhere for everyone to go!"

Emily thought hard. What they needed was a sheltered place out of the way of the avalanche, big enough for all the villagers. Suddenly she had an idea. She leaned forward and whispered to Crystal, "Do you think the villagers could hide in the cave?"

He tossed his head, making the bells on his reins jingle. "That's a great idea! Tell Sasha quickly."

"Sasha! Can we take the villagers to your secret cave? It's so big—everyone can be safe there, and the waterfall will shield us from the snow."

"But the path is so narrow," Sasha said doubtfully. "I'm not sure we can get everyone up there."

"There's nowhere else! We have to, Sasha. And we must go quickly. Look, that cloud of snow is getting bigger and bigger!"

Sasha looked up at the mountain and gasped when she saw how much closer the avalanche was. She turned Clover around to face the crowd and stood up in her stirrups.

"Listen, everyone!" she shouted. But her voice was too small for the scared villagers to hear.

Crystal stamped his front hoof and neighed as loudly as he could. At once everyone stopped and looked at them. Emily patted his neck gratefully.

Sasha shouted, "We have to get away from the village. There's a mountain cave not far away where we can all shelter from the avalanche. We'll show you!"

The villagers looked unsure. Emily guessed they didn't know about the cave behind the waterfall.

"Please!" Sasha begged. "There's no time to lose!"

"She's right," said a woman. "We don't have time to talk about it. If Sasha knows a good place to shelter, we should go."

A very old man with a long white beard stepped forward, leaning heavily on a walking stick. "Is it behind a waterfall?" he asked Sasha.

"With lots of paintings?"

Sasha nodded.

The old man beamed. "Then you've found the secret cave! I went there once, many years ago. I never thought anyone would find it again." He faced the crowd. "Follow Sasha, everyone!"

Sasha wheeled Clover around and pointed to the path that led up the mountain. "Come on! It's this way!"

The villagers started to stream out of the village square. Emily saw Sasha's parents run up with Arin. "Sasha!" called Sasha's mother. "Take Arin with you. Your father and I need to take the cattle to the sheltered pasture on the far side of the village, and then we'll follow you." She lifted Arin up to sit on Clover's back in front of Sasha. "Good-bye! Look after your little brother, Sasha."

Arin turned around to try and call after his

mother, but she'd already hurried off with Sasha's father to get the cattle to safety. Gregor the farmhand was heading that way, too, but when he saw them, he stopped and stroked Crystal's mane. Crystal snorted with pleasure. Gregor's eyes were twinkling, but he spoke seriously. "Don't be scared, Emily. Whatever happens, remember you and Crystal are a team. You can do anything!" Then he turned and strode off. Emily stared after him for a moment, then wheeled Crystal around to face the mountain and their journey.

Emily and Sasha set off, leading the villagers up the path to the cave. Emily patted Crystal's neck. "Come on, boy, you can do it. I know you're tired, but we have to go quickly."

"Don't worry." Crystal gave a confident neigh. "Rescue work like this is what snow ponies are bred for, Emily. You just concentrate on keeping everyone together."

Sasha was struggling with Arin. "Sit still!" she scolded.

"We've left Ivar behind!" Arin cried. "I'm going back to get him!"

Before Sasha could say anything, he jumped down from Clover's back. Emily saw the little boy pushing his way through the crowd, and she quickly turned Crystal around to stop him. But it was too late.

He had vanished!

Chapter Seven

"Oh no!" gasped Sasha.

Emily steered Crystal alongside Clover. "Don't panic!" she told her friend. She thought fast. "Sasha, you'll have to keep going to the cave. You're the only person who knows the way. Crystal and I will go back and get Arin."

"But my mother told me to take care of him," Sasha said miserably.

"I know, but I can't guide everyone, Sasha. I've only been to the cave once, and I might not remember the way. But if I go and find Arin, we'll be able to follow your footprints in the snow. Trust me, Crystal and I will find him for you."

Sasha nodded. "Okay. Good luck!"

"We'll be back soon!" Emily wheeled Crystal around, and they set off down the mountain. They weaved their way through the villagers, searching for Arin in every group. Emily twisted her fingers into Crystal's mane as they galloped down the slippery path. Crystal was going as fast as he could, his hooves expertly finding a grip on the snowy track.

But it was no good. Arin was nowhere to be seen.

"He must have gone back to the farm," puffed Emily. "I think we've found who needs our help, don't you?"

"Definitely!" Crystal agreed. He twitched his ears and galloped even faster. "I can hear the avalanche getting closer—the trees on the mountain will slow it for a while, but we haven't got long. Hold tight!"

They raced through the village. Everywhere was deserted, silent except for the rumbling snow that got louder and louder. Crystal skidded to a halt in front of the farmhouse, scattering snow under his hooves.

"Arin!" Emily jumped out of the saddle and shouted as loud as she could. "Arin, it's me, Emily!"

"Maybe he's in the stable," Crystal suggested.

Emily led him over to the barn. The door was open, but inside the stable was empty.

Where was Arin?

Then Emily heard a whimpering noise coming

from the corner of the stable. It sounded as if it was coming from under the floor.

"The apple cellar!" she cried.

She ran over and peered down the slope into the apple cellar. It was dark and gloomy, and Emily couldn't see anything from there, but the whimpering was definitely louder.

"Come on," said Crystal, walking past Emily and stepping carefully down the slope. He ducked his head to avoid the low ceiling, making the silver bells on his bridle jingle.

Emily followed him, feeling very glad she had her pony friend with her. He was so brave!

"Emily!" As Emily's eyes got used to the shadows in the cellar, she saw Arin curled up in the corner with his arms around Ivar. "I'm sorry I ran off, but I couldn't leave Ivar behind."

"We need to go to the cave!" Emily told him.

"The avalanche is coming—"

At that moment, the dull rumbling noise in the background suddenly got louder—and louder! The walls of the stable started to shake.

"We're too late!" Crystal whinnied. "Emily, lie down and cover your head, in case the snow makes the walls collapse! Get Arin and Ivar down, too."

Emily grabbed Arin and pulled him down beside her. "Don't worry, Arin. We're safe, but we have to lie down. Can you get Ivar to lie down as well?"

Arin was too scared to argue, and Ivar seemed to know what he ought to do anyway. As soon as Arin lay down, the big dog lay down next to him. He rested his head on the little boy's back as if he was protecting him.

"Ooof!" muttered Arin. "You're heavy, Ivar."

Crystal stood over the little group as the

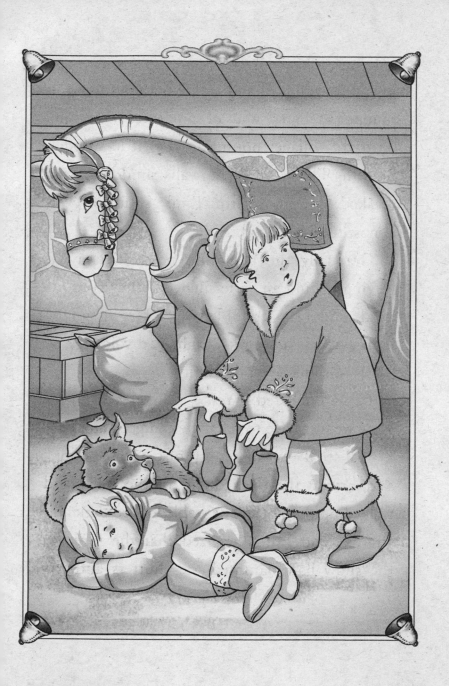

avalanche rumbled and crashed around them. It sounded as if great walls of snow were whooshing onto the village, pounding the little wooden building like waves. The walls shuddered and creaked, but stood firm. Emily shut her eyes, almost too scared to breathe.

Gradually the rumbling noise died away, leaving behind an eerie silence. Arin raised his head, and Ivar scrambled up. "Has it gone?" Arin asked in a squeaky, frightened voice.

"I—I think so," said Emily.

Crystal snorted. "Yes. I think it's stopped. Now we just have to see if we can get out."

"I'll see if we can get out of the stable door," said Emily. She ducked out of the cellar and walked up the slope. The stable looked dark and strange, and Emily realized that the force of the snow had slammed the shutters and the door shut. She pushed at the big wooden door. It was stuck fast! The snow was piled up outside it. She rattled the latch and threw herself at the door, again and again. It made no difference. They were trapped!

Crystal, Arin, and Ivar were standing at the top of the slope when Emily turned around. "Can't we get out?" Arin asked, his voice shaking.

"I'm sure we can. Don't worry." Emily was trying to be brave for Arin's sake, but she didn't know how they were going to get out of the stable.

"Is there another way out?" whinnied Crystal. "This door is on the side nearest the mountain, so this is where most of the snow will be. Can we get out on the far side, where the apple cellar is?"

"Why is Crystal whinnying so much?" Arin said. "Is he scared, too?"

Emily gave him a hug. She'd forgotten that to Arin, Crystal's good ideas would just sound like pony noises! "He's trying to cheer us up. Come on, Arin. Let's go and look for another way out." She led the way back into the apple cellar, then stared around at the walls. There was a small door set in the wall, just above the floor level. "Maybe we can get out there!" she said, pointing.

"This is where we put the apples into the cellar," Arin explained as they ran over to it. "We bring the baskets in from the orchard this way."

"And this side of the stable is farthest from the mountain and the avalanche," Emily realized. "There shouldn't be so much snow here." She stretched up to the latch, but it was at the top of the door, and she couldn't reach it. "Arin, if I give you a piggyback, could you reach up and undo the latch for us?"

Arin nodded.

Emily ducked down for the little boy to clamber onto her back, then straightened up as Arin puffed and stretched above her.

"Done it!" he cried at last, tugging on the handle. With a loud creaking noise the little door swung open. Luckily it opened inward, so they didn't have to push against the snow.

"Uuurgh!" Emily spluttered, as a load of wet snow fell on her face. She set Arin down, and tried to dig out some of the snow at the bottom of the doorway. It wasn't packed solid, but it still looked like a long and difficult job. Emily was just looking around for a spade when she noticed Ivar sniffing excitedly at the snow.

"I think Ivar wants to help," Crystal said. "I bet he's good at digging."

"Go on, boy!" shouted Arin, who had noticed his dog as well. "Get us out of here!"

Ivar let out a joyful woof and started digging at the snow with his huge front paws. Crystal helped, too, scraping with his front hoof. Emily and Arin cleared the loose snow back into the apple cellar, using a shovel from Clover's stable.

Suddenly Ivar gave a triumphant yelp. He'd dug all the way through! A bright white light filtered down into the cellar through the narrow tunnel.

"Well done, Ivar! Good boy!" Arin and Emily shouted as Ivar's wagging tail disappeared out of the hole.

"Your turn, Arin!" Emily gave him a boost,

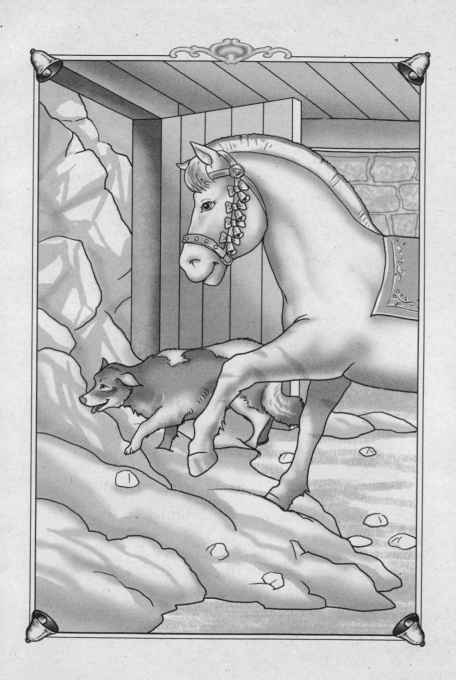

and he struggled up, reaching for the hole. She tried to lift him higher, but her arms were aching.

"I'm slipping," Arin squeaked, his voice rising in panic.

Emily felt Crystal's bristly mane tickle her cheek as he came up beside her. He nudged Arin up with his nose. "Thanks, Crystal!" Emily puffed. Peering up through the tunnel, she saw Ivar gently grab Arin's collar in his teeth to haul the little boy out.

"Up you go, Emily," snorted Crystal. "If you can widen the hole from the top, I can get out, too."

With Crystal as a step up it was easy for Emily to scramble out of Ivar's tunnel. It was like climbing out of a rabbit hole! Then she, Arin, and Ivar set to work to make the hole big enough for Crystal. At last he was able to squeeze through, bursting into the open with a joyful neigh.

Emily threw her arms around him. They'd done it!

Chapter Eight

"We did it! We did it!" Emily cried. Ivar jumped up to lick her face, and she hugged him, too. Then she turned to hug Arin, but to her dismay he had started to cry. "Arin! It's all right, we're safe now!"

"Sasha's going to be so mad at me!" Arin wailed. "And my mom and dad. But I couldn't leave Ivar behind!"

"Don't worry." Emily patted him on the back. "Everyone will be waiting for you at the cave." *At least, I hope they are,* she thought anxiously. Had Sasha managed to get them there before the avalanche struck? "They'll be so glad to see you, I'm sure they won't be angry. Come on, let's go and find them."

Emily helped Arin scramble up onto Crystal's back, and then she jumped up behind him. Ivar trotted along beside them as they set off through the village again. It all looked so strange! Many of the houses were half buried in snow, and there were lots of branches scattered around. They must have been broken off trees farther up the mountain and carried along by the avalanche. It looked as if there would be a lot of digging out and cleaning up to do, but the log cabins were so sturdy that no real damage had been done.

"Do you think we'll be able to find the mountain path again?" Emily whispered to Crystal.

"I'll do my best," said Crystal, tossing his head.

The snow was so deep now that it came up to Crystal's tummy. "Hold on tight," he snorted, and Emily wrapped her arms around Arin as the pony plunged through the snow. Emily turned around and saw Ivar bounding in and out of Crystal's trail.

"This is where the path starts," Emily said when they reached the pine forest. "But I can't see any footprints."

"The avalanche must have covered them," said Crystal.

Emily's heart sank. She had hoped they would be able to follow the tracks left by the villagers. They had to find the cave. Arin's family would be so worried about him! How else could they find their way to the frozen waterfall?

"Wait!" she cried. "What about the things in the forest that Sasha showed us this morning? We saw the patch of gentians first, and they were in a ring of silver birch trees."

Crystal snorted, and started to trot up through the trees. "Right," he puffed. "I'll watch out for silver birch trees."

"There are some silver trees," Arin said, a little farther on.

Emily hugged him. "Well spotted, Arin! We must be going the right way! Now we have to find a rock that's shaped like a cat."

Looking out for the landmarks seemed to stop Arin from worrying about his mom and dad. Emily peered through the shadowy trees, holding the reins loosely so that Crystal could pick his way through the snow. Suddenly a familiar shape loomed ahead.

"Look!" cried Emily. "There's the rock shaped like a cat."

Crystal broke into a trot. The snow was thinner now, and they could see something sparkling ahead through the trees.

They reached the edge of the forest, and there was the waterfall, sparkling in the sunshine. And standing in front of it was Sasha!

"Sasha!" cried Arin. He slipped down from Crystal's back and ran over to his sister. "I'll never run away again, I promise!"

Sasha hugged him tight. "I thought you'd been caught in the avalanche! Oh, Arin, I'm sorry I was annoyed at you." Then she turned and called into the cave. "They're here! Emily and Arin are here!"

Arin's parents rushed out from behind the waterfall. His father scooped him up and held him close, while his mother took turns kissing him and telling him off. "I never thought we'd get you back! Don't you ever frighten me like that again, Arin!"

Arin wriggled, pretending to be embarrassed but really enjoying all the fuss.

The other villagers came out, too, smiling and laughing—now that Emily and Arin had arrived, everyone was safe.

"We've had a lucky escape, thanks to you two," said the old man who'd known about the cave. "And it's wonderful to find this place again!"

Sasha's father put down Arin and turned to Emily. "How did the village look?" he asked.

"There's a lot of snow," Emily told him, "and most of the houses are half buried, but none of them has been knocked down."

"Did you hear that?" Sasha's father turned to his neighbors. "The avalanche hasn't destroyed the town. I think we should go ahead with the rest of Spring Festival and celebrate our lucky escape!"

Emily smiled, thinking how much fun it would be to share in the festival. But suddenly the air began to fill with sparkling crystals. Was it starting to snow again? She looked up, but the sky was a clear, bright, springtime blue.

Crystal whinnied loudly. "The magic carousel is pulling us back, Emily! It's time to go! Say good-bye, quick!"

Emily gave Sasha a hug and climbed up onto Crystal's back. "I have to go. Thank you for showing me the cave, Sasha! I've got to go back to my own village now," she explained. "Don't worry, Crystal will look after me!"

"Good-bye!" called Sasha. "Come back and visit us soon!"

Crystal trotted off between the trees, and

Emily waved back to her friends. The sparkling crystals grew thicker, hiding the forest in a twinkling rainbow. Emily felt as if she and Crystal were galloping through a snow cloud! Then the sparkles faded away and Emily found herself back on the Magic Pony Carousel. The bells on Crystal's harness jingled one last time as the ride slowed to a stop.

Emily slipped from Crystal's saddle, feeling dazed. She was wearing her own clothes again, jeans and her pink denim jacket. She ran her hand down Crystal's mane. Instead of warm bristles, she felt carved wood beneath her fingers. He was a carousel pony again. "Good-bye, Crystal," she whispered. "Thank you for my adventure!"

She stepped off the carousel, and saw Jane and Max waving.

"Max!" Emily ran over and gave him a big hug.

Max looked a bit surprised. "Watch out for my balloon!" he yelped. Emily laughed. She was going to be much nicer to Max from now on. Little brothers could be a pain sometimes, but they were very special.

As Max wriggled free, Emily heard a tinkling sound—just like bells. She looked down and saw a beautiful yellow ribbon tied around her wrist, with two tiny silver bells on it. Emily shook the bells in delight. She knew it was a present from the carousel, to make sure she always remembered her magical adventure.

"Did you enjoy your ride on the carousel?" Jane asked.

"Oh yes! It was wonderful!" Emily beamed at her sister, knowing that she could never tell her what had really happened. Jane would never believe that she'd gone on a magical pony ride to a land of ice and snow and helped rescue a

mountain village from an avalanche! But Emily knew it had happened. Her beautiful, brave Crystal had been real, and she would never forget their time together.

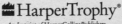